The Cat Who Smelled Murder

Sky Valley Cozy Mystery Cat Series
Book 1

By: William Jarvis

Yap Kee Chong

8345 NW 66 ST #B7885

Miami, FL 33166

Createspace

Copyright 2015

Get Notice of Our New Releases Here!

http://eepurl.com/7jbzn

Part 2 – Who Is Killing, Kitten?

Part 3 – The Cat Who Saved Me

Sky Valley Cozy Mystery Cat Series Box Set

Contents

CHAPTER 1
SHE DOESN'T WANT TO BE ALONE

Emmy looked at herself in the mirror and fixed one of her pearl earrings in place. She never really liked dressing up like she was going to a convention of some sort, but tonight was a special night. So special, in fact, that her father, Troy Byrne, decided to hold a party, a far cry from his *spending time alone with Audrina* phase, now that they could still be considered newlyweds.

He's actually signed a new business deal, one about selling calligraphy pens and materials. It's a hobby that Emmy's always been interested in, and she was happy her father was back on track again. It has been a while after the whole Lena McMahon fiasco, anyway.

You see, their lives changed dramatically over a year ago when Emmy came back from Paris. Apparently, Lena McMahon, former Chief Police Officer of the Sky Valley Jail, and Tryke Miller, Troy's former business rival, held a grudge against Troy. Lena has been in love with him ever since they were in high school, and she wasn't able to get over the fact that Troy married Emmy's mother. From then on, she plotted revenge against him, and when she realized that Tryke was also in love with Emmy's mother and hated Troy for being able to get everything he wanted, the two of them decided to ruin Troy's life—and Emmy's, too.

Because Tryke's daughter, Annabeth, died because of his evil plans, he became more determined to ruin Troy. In fact, a few more people died in the process, including Daniel's ex-girlfriend, Ruby; Annabeth's husband, Matt; and even Ruby's husband, Edward. It was all so crazy until Emmy figured out the truth and drove Lena away from Sky Valley. Since then, her father hasn't really ventured into business anymore, but today was different.

Emmy feels like it's a good time to start anew, especially because life had been pretty eventful in the past couple of months. Sometimes, she still couldn't believe that she was able to help a ghost named Lucy, a 15-year-old girl who got her whole life thwarted. Now, she feels that she's finally ready to live a life that's more "normal," without thinking about a lot. She needs it, too, especially because she and Dan are now parents to a baby girl named Charlize.

Just then, Daniel entered the room and hugged Emmy from behind. "Is my lovely wife ready?"

Emmy grinned and faced Daniel before kissing him on the lips. "You look sharp yourself." She said, and knew that Daniel really did. He looked amazing in his black suit, with matching silver-gray tie.

"Don't want to embarrass Troy, you know." He quipped. "This is his comeback in the world of business."

"I know." Emmy smiled. "I'm really nervous, though...I mean, I hope everything goes well. I want everything to go well."

"And there you go worrying again," Daniel said and squeezed her hand. "Everything's going to be okay." He said.

They shared a smile and walked hand in hand to the other room where their daughter, Charlize, and her babysitter, Bella, were staying. Dan and Emmy thought that Bella's a really nice, responsible young girl of seventeen. She was always just quiet, and would smile at them nicely. She never makes Charlize cry, and Charlize obviously loves her a lot, too.

Emmy met Bella while she was in her Fashion Studio one day. She often brought Charlize to work back then and when Bella offered to babysit, she agreed. Of course, she looked at Bella's credentials, too, but the girl really had it in her. And Emmy saw how caring she was with Charlize, so now, she and Dan feel confident to let her take care of the baby when they had to work or go somewhere, just like tonight.

"So, you all right, Bella?" Emmy asked.

"Yes, everything's good." Bella smiled, and Emmy thought that if she actually had a sister, she'd want Bella to be that girl. She was just so charming, but Wendy, their 1-year-old Maine Coon, didn't really like her so much. This was unusual, Emmy thought, because Wendy liked almost everyone—but maybe there really are some people whom cats would never be fond of.

"Don't forget to call us if anything, okay?" Emmy told her. "And, don't forget to give her milk before nine, she usually gets hungry...or needy," she laughed and went on, "by that time."

"We'll be okay, don't worry." Bella smiled. "You guys enjoy your night."

"We'll be back before you know it." Emmy smiled at her and just as they were about to leave the house, their cat, Wendy, started to meow so loud that Emmy and Dan were confused.

"You fed her, right?" Emmy asked Daniel.

"Yeah, she just ate a few minutes ago. There's still some food in her bowl."

"But what's the problem, Wendy?" Emmy asked as she scooped Wendy from the floor. Wendy was still meowing. *Mehwww-mehwwwww-mehwwwww.* "What is it, girl?"

"I feel like she doesn't want to be alone," Daniel said and carried Wendy. She instantly purred. "See?" He said. "The 'I want to be your baby' vibes are strong!"

Emmy laughed as she petted Wendy. "Honey, we have to go."

Meooooowrrrrrrr! Wendy uttered loudly as if saying "no."

"What do we do now?" Emmy asked. "You think we should bring her with us?"

"Yeah, why not?"

Emmy pursed her lips then petted Wendy. "Will you be a good girl?"

Wendy answered in the form of purring.

"I guess that's your answer." Daniel smiled.

"Oh well, come on, then," Emmy said and carried Wendy, not minding her fur on her dress.

Daniel kissed Charlize whom Bella was carrying. "We'll see you both in a few." He smiled and helped Emmy as they both went out of the house.

It feels like it's going to be a good night, Emmy thought. Or was she wishing for too much?

The Cat Who Smelled Murder #1

Cats are some of the best creatures on earth. They're smart, interesting, and well...they could be manipulative, too.

Did you know that cats can adjust their meows and purrs to how they want their "humans" to see them? Yep, they're smart like that—especially when there's a baby in the house and they feel like their role in your life is threatened. This is because they can actually mimic the sounds they hear, especially the sounds a baby makes. This way, they get your attention right away and you could easily give them what they want.

Pretty nasty, huh?

CHAPTER 2
PARTY ANIMALS

When Daniel and Emmy arrived at the Byrne's residence, they noticed that the place looked splendid. The rose bushes were in full bloom, and there were silver and pink balloons everywhere. In fact, Wendy seemed to be so excited that she decided to pop one of those balloons using her paw.

"Wendy!" Emmy said as she saw Wendy attacking one of the balloons, but she was too late because Wendy already popped one. "Oh, you naughty, naughty kitten!" She said as she picked Wendy up and kissed her on the nose. "I told you to behave!" She put Wendy down and she just purled around her leg while trying to get Daniel's attention.

"She's becoming nasty." Daniel quipped and they both laughed.

"You know," Just then, they heard Audrina coming near them, "If you guys weren't married, you'd be relegated to crazy cat people status. I mean, that's just a thought, you know..." She smiled at them, and Emmy noticed how she's gotten even more beautiful, with her brown and blonde-streaked hair and modern housewife demeanor.

"Looking good, step-mother." Emmy grinned.

Audrina swatted her lightly on the arm. "Oh, you shut up." She raised an eyebrow. She and Audrina's dad, Troy, got married six months ago and it was one of the best times in her life. She was glad that she had Emmy as a friend, and as a step-daughter, no matter how weird the consequences were. "You look amazing yourself!"

"Any news?" Emmy asked. "Am I getting a step-sibling soon?"

"NO!" Audrina said a little too loudly. "Sorry, I mean…that's not really in our plans right now, with all this traveling and stuff, it's kind of not possible." She said. "How's little Charlize doing? You still have the same babysitter?"

"Yeah, Bella's amazing with her," Emmy said. "She's great with Charlize but not with Wendy. We had to bring her because she kept on crying, it's like she didn't want to be home with them. She's even worse than Charlize, I'm telling you."

"Oh, poor darling Wendy doesn't like sweet Bella?" Audrina said as she knelt down to pet Wendy, whom she also spent a lot of time with during the past couple of months, especially when they were still trying to help Lucy the ghost.

"Nah," Emmy said, "I actually wonder why coz' you know Wendy's a sweet and friendly cat…" One of the waiters hired for the event then gave them their glasses of champagne. "Thanks!" Emmy said and smiled before Audrina took her glass from her.

"No drinking for you!" Audrina said. "You're still breastfeeding, you know."

Emmy laughed. "Such a sweet grandmother."

They all laughed.

"Where's Troy, then?" Daniel asked. "I can't wait to see the man! He hasn't told us much about this new business partner of his. Have you met him?"

"Once, yeah. His name's Caleb." Audrina replied. "He's…pretty decent."

Emmy raised an eyebrow. "What does that even mean?"

Audrina shrugged as she drank some champagne. "I don't know, I mean, he's pretty nice but…there's something off about him. Like, all I know is that he's from New York, was on top of his class at Stanford, and has been all over the world, too. He has this gorgeous wife—like Miranda Kerr levels—but he's kind of reclusive about his past, so I really don't know what to think about that. I mean, with our experiences and all, it's so hard to trust already, but you know how your father is…"

"Always so trusting." Emmy took a deep breath. "Now this makes me want to meet this man even more."

"Troy's a good guy," Daniel said, "He just trusts so quickly, but maybe we should give this to him, especially since it's his comeback in the line of business. But, if we see odd signs, we should—"

"Go sleuthing again, eh?" Emmy asked with a smile on her face. She then saw her father making his way towards them, some canapés in hand.

"Oh, there you are!" He greeted as he gave each of them some canapés and returned the tray to one of the waiters. "I'm so glad you made it."

"We're glad, too, daddy," Emmy said as she kissed him on the cheek. "We have a lot to talk about."

The Cat Who Smelled Murder #1

No one can deny the fact that cats are big attention seekers. If their pack was the Brady Bunch, they'd all be Marcia—always "me, me, me."

Some even say that people don't really own cats—cats own people. Cats have this great, big power over people that makes it hard for people to ignore them. They often get what they want because if they don't, a lot of craziness will ensue.

But, more often than not, there's a reason why cats try to get people's attention. It's often a sign that they're hungry, they need to pee, they need to take a dump...or they just want to be petted.

Just like babies, cats want to feel that their parents' attention is on them. They want to know that they matter, that their existence is important. They want to know that they're not just treated as cats, but as equals.

Again, cats are smart creatures—they know what they want, they know what to do.

But that doesn't mean that they no longer need you.

CHAPTER 3
JUMPING' JUMPIN'

"Hey, I see you brought little Wendy here..." Troy said as he petted Wendy on the head. Wendy purred. She's always been affectionate with Troy, probably knowing that he's her "grandfather."

"Yeah, she doesn't want to be home with Bella and Charlize."

"She doesn't like Bella..." Daniel added. "That's why you and Audrina should go visit sometime. Maybe next Sunday?"

"Yeah, that sounds good," Troy said. "You barely visit, too, you know?"

"Sorry, we've just been crazy busy," Daniel said. "I have these really demanding clients from Florida who want to put up a cozy reading nook slash café near Reynolds Square. They have all the papers ready and they want to make sure the place looks great...you know the deal." He said. "And Emmy here's been getting a lot of orders for her gowns, there's even this one woman who wants her to make a gown that's inspired by Kate Middleton's wedding dress."

"Oh don't even get me started on that." Emmy smiled and thanked the waiter for giving her a glass of water. She drank some water and went on. "She says she wants to get married in like, three months, and she wants to mimic Kate's gown, but, of course, that couldn't happen unless I want to be tagged for copyright infringement and all that. But anyway, I'm trying to make her understand that that's the case so let's hope she does. Anyway...dad, it's you who has a lot to tell us!" She patted her father on the arm. "Who's this mystery business partner of yours?"

"Oh, he's Caleb Roberts. You'll meet him later. He's great. He's a really smart guy, he studied at Stanford, has been to Nice, Paris, Hawaii, and London, amongst a lot of places, and he knows what he's doing. I think that's the most important part. He's into the whole importing business."

"Which is a far cry from what you used to do," Emmy said. "I mean, why the sudden change of interest? You could have just gotten back to putting up your own restaurant, or maybe just a coffee shop or so. Don't you think it's Time for Coffee once again? I mean, you can do it without this partner of yours. I'm pretty sure Audrina could help. We could help."

"Honey, thanks for your vote of confidence," Troy said, "but it's not as simple as that. We can't just tell everyone that I'm getting back to the same old business. You know how tainted my name already is."

"But dad, you know that none of it was your fault, right?" Emmy asked.

"That's what I keep on saying." Audrina nodded her head and drank some champagne. "But your father never listens."

"I never listen because I know that even if we know the truth, I'm still at fault because I was negligent. If I wasn't negligent, Jimmy wouldn't have made his way inside Time for Coffee. If I wasn't negligent, Annabeth probably would still be alive. I'm not really berating myself for this anymore but...you know...it's better to be safe rather than sorry. I couldn't risk the lives of a lot of people anymore. So, I thought if we could just work on developing a line of silverware and other kitchen furniture, then that would be great. Those things are useful, especially here in Sky Valley."

"But where did you even meet him?" Emmy asked.

"I met him at one of these seminars that I attended and he said that he has heard about me, but he believes it's high time for a comeback. In another line, of course, and I thought why not? I missed doing business. It's been too long. I just couldn't go back to the cooking line yet."

"And you didn't find that to be suspicious?" Emmy said as Wendy nibbled on some cat chow on the ground. They often bring cat chow or kibbles with them whenever Wendy wanted to come with them.

"Why would it be suspicious?" Troy asked. "Look, I know life's been tough for all of us in the past year or two but that doesn't necessarily mean that we could no longer trust anyone."

"I know, dad," Emmy said, "but I guess we also have to be a bit more careful. At least, do a background check or something. I trust you, dad, but we have to be more careful."

"And I thank you, Emmy," he said, "but you have to trust me with this. I got this."

Emmy sighed. "Dad—"

But before she could say another word, her father spoke again. "Oh, look, there he is."

RAWWWRRRRR GRRRRRROOWOWWWWWLLLLSSSSSSS

And it was just a matter of seconds before Wendy growled so loud that the throng of people around them wondered what was going on. Wendy then found the man Troy was talking about—a tall man, wearing a silvery-gray suit, with an air of confidence and intelligence about him—then she jumped on him, growling and using her claws with all her might.

The Cat Who Smelled Murder #1

They say that cats are also instinctive creatures, but some humans just fail to realize the signals that cats give until it's too late.

Take, for instance, a cat named Faith, who once lived in St. Augustine's Abbey in the late '30's to early '40's. She was once just a cat who loitered around the church and when the Parishioner Henry Ross realized that Faith attended all his services, he decided to take her in and take care of her.

But as the war was around, there was a threat that the church would be bombed—and Faith knew this ahead of anyone else. In fact, she kept going down to the basement of the church and Henry didn't know what she was doing. He thought she was just trying to get attention, so he let her be.

And then a few days after that, the church was bombed, and the rescuers said that there's no chance that Faith would have survived. Henry didn't want to give up right away because he loved Faith a lot and wanted to know that she was alive. So, he made his way to the basement and found out that not only was Faith alive, she also had some kittens—her children—with her. The reason why she kept going to the basement was because she wanted to save her children, as she knew that something terrible was going to happen.

From then on, Ross promised to take care of her and her kittens—until Faith died in 1945 and her death became worldwide news. People mourned and remembered the cat who was once deemed as the Bravest Cat in the World.

You see what could happen if people only knew how to listen to cats?

CHAPTER 4
SHE HATES ME

"Wendy!" Daniel and Emmy called out as they saw what Wendy did. "Come here!" Daniel said and took Wendy away from Caleb Roberts, who looked just as appalled as everyone. "Sorry, man, she's just—,"He said as he took down the still growling Wendy from Caleb's body, "—she's going through a rough time, sorry."

"We're really sorry," Emmy said as she took Wendy from Daniel. "She's not really like that most of the time." She petted Wendy to try to calm her down, but she was still hissing to no avail. "Wendy, stop!"'s

But Wendy just got out of Emmy's grasp and circled Caleb before pooping as fast as she could on the ground and running inside The Byrnes' house.

"Oh my goodness," Emmy muttered, "I have no idea what just happened."

***

Emmy washed her hands as Daniel made his way towards her. After the unfortunate incident in the garden, they tried to clean up the mess and said sorry to everyone. The party still went on, though, but on the other side of the garden. Daniel also helped Wendy go to sleep in Emmy's old room where she usually stays when they visit Troy and Audrina.

"She okay?" Emmy asked Daniel. They were now in the kitchen with Audrina, who was sipping some tea. "I wonder what's wrong with her. I called the vet already, but she said that Wendy's probably just having jealousy issues but I mean, she's with us and Charlize is not even here. I'd bring her to the vet tomorrow. But I don't know...it probably has something to do with that Caleb guy."

"Uh-huh," Audrina said, "Cats can smell bad people, you know? I had this cat once, his name was Howie and while I was vacationing at my grandmother's house, he kept hissing and growling one afternoon and surprise! There was this man at the window who was trying to get inside the house, he's this guy who's known in the community as a thief and thanks to Howie, grandpa was able to beat him up and bring him to the police."

"I get your point, Audrina," Daniel said, "But we really just can't go and tell Troy that Caleb's this total bad guy. We'll work on that, though. Let me talk to him." He kissed Emmy on the forehead and made his way to the garden where the party was in full swing.

Emmy took a deep breath as she drank some water and sat next to Audrina. "I have a terrible feeling about this. I wish dad would listen to me."

"Yeah, I know," Audrina said, "But we have to take things slowly. Dan's right when he said we can't just tell Troy that he's wrong yet again and this Caleb person is a bad guy. We have to sort of, strategize a bit."

"But if dad's life would be in danger—"

Their conversation was cut short because right at that moment, Caleb came in the room. "Oh, hey," He said, "Do you know where the toilet is?"

"Just to your right," Emmy answered, "There's this curtain there and it'll lead you to a door...anyway," she went on, "I'm really sorry again for what Wendy did. I mean, if you knew her, you'd know she's not really like that. She's probably just...stressed."

Caleb laughed, "Nah, she probably hates me."

"Really, now?" Emmy raised an eyebrow. "Does she have any reason to hate you, Mr. Caleb Roberts, huh?"

Caleb looked her in the eyes and took a deep breath before speaking. "Well, Miss Emilia Byrne, I don't think so." He said, "Or wait...maybe, your Wendy just smelled the scent of my Olivia."

"Your Olivia?"

"She's my cat. My wife's, actually, but she's pretty cool."

"Oh," Emmy said and took a deep breath, "I'm sure she is. Just like you."

Caleb laughed, "I'm not." He said, "Why don't you two go out and join us? It's a party, you shouldn't be spending all your time here, you know?"

"Yeah, we're fine," Audrina said. "We'll be there in a bit."

"Great, 'coz we're planning a giveaway. We have this car to give to the attendees, one of you might win." He smiled, "Kidding, of course. But, you know, we have stuff to give away. I'll see you?"

Emmy just raised an eyebrow as an answer and when they were sure that Caleb was no longer nearby, she and Audrina shared a look.

"He's charming," Audrina said.

"I know," Emmy said. "And you know what that means, right?"

Audrina nodded her head. "Charming usually means deceptive. We know what to do."

Emmy took a deep breath and then she felt so dizzy like she was no longer where she was.

The Cat Who Smelled Murder #1

Cats don't only poop when they have to, they also do it when they want to.

The reason they do this is because they want to insult some of the people around them. Just imagine another person pooping on you, or near you. It's definitely not a great feeling, right?

Well, cats think the same way. They know that other people won't be able to screw them over, or make them feel bad about themselves when they've already marked their territory.

In a way, pooping is their way of telling you to back off...or else you'll be dead.

CHAPTER 5
INTO THE PAST AND BEYOND

Emmy was so dizzy. She never felt this way in a long time, not even when she was pregnant with Charlize. The last time she felt this way was when she was having those dreams involving Annabeth and Ruby, allowing her to help them to avenge and figure out the truth about their deaths.

She also felt this way when Lucy was around, and she really didn't want to deal with any ghosts anymore, but she had no idea what was happening. It was like a big, black cloud of smoke was around her head and she was hearing things that no other people could.

Caleb, I love you. I love you so much my heart is going to break. You just have no idea, do you?

Why don't you just shut up? It was Caleb's voice, and he was so angry, so angry that Emmy felt his anger seethe towards her; like it was so real; so raw.

Shut up already.

But what were you doing with her? Why were you calling her?

That's none of your business, Marissa. We work together. That's that.

Yeah? But why do you often go out together? Why can't you leave each other alone?!

You're insane. Back off, or something will happen.

No, Caleb—

Marissa, stop—

I will not stop! I haven't been with you in a while and whenever we're together, you're acting like you just want to be somewhere else! You want me to be...be this person who I'm not—

No, Marissa, you're turning me into the person I don't want to be!

What the hell does that mean?!

It means what it means!

Are you going to kill me?!

Marissa, stop!

No, you stop! You're not going to do this!

Marissa! There was an evident fear in his voice; fear mixed with anger; fear that could kill.

Caleb, stop!

And then there was a sound of something colliding, like two large items being pitted together. There was an explosion. And there was the voice of Audrina asking Emmy if she was okay.

"Hey, hey, what's going on?" Audrina asked.

Emmy looked at her and realized that she was still in the kitchen and Audrina was holding her, trying to help her get up. "Are you okay?"

"Yeah, I was just...I don't know, Audrina, I had a vision."

"A vision?" Audrina asked just as Wendy made her way towards Emmy and purled around her leg. "What do you mean?"

"I heard things. I mean...this already happened before but in the form of dreams...you know, about Annabeth and Ruby, but this time...this time it just felt so real, like I was there. My head just felt like it was going to explode and there those visions were."

"What did you see?"

"It's a woman and a man...the man was Caleb and he was younger and the woman's name was Marissa and she was saying something about another woman, saying that Caleb shouldn't have been calling her...Audrina, something's wrong with that man."

"This is what I'm talking about."

"What's going on?" Caleb then asked. "You girls okay?"

"Yeah, we're fine," Audrina answered abruptly.

"Emmy, you look pale," Caleb said. "Should I call your husband or—"

"I'm fine," Emmy stated.

"She's fine," Audrina said. "Just—"

Before any of them could say another word, Wendy hissed yet again and got all of their attention.

"What is it, Wendy?" Emmy asked. Then they heard the sounds of police car sirens ringing. In fact, they have been ringing for a while but they didn't realize it earlier because they were too busy tending to Emmy, wondering about what happened.

"What's going on?" Caleb asked.

"Maybe we should be asking you that—"

Just then, Troy and Daniel came back to the house with policemen behind them. Emmy saw Sara, her friend from the police station and wondered what was going on.

"Sara, what's this?" She asked.

"What's going on?" Caleb asked again, nerves more evident this time. "Did something go wrong outside?"

"Not outside, Mr. Roberts, no," Sara answered. "But, unfortunately, we received a call from your home, and when we went there..." She paused and took a deep breath, obviously collecting her thoughts. "We're sorry, Mr. Roberts, but your wife, Rose, is dead."

"What?" Caleb asked. "I—I don't understand—"

"There was a suicide note, but we believe there's something more to this and we have to take you in for questioning. Sorry to interrupt the party. You have the right to remain silent, and the right to an attorney. Everything you say may be used against you, so—"

Sara's words drowned in Emmy's thoughts because all she could see was her father's face. There was a look of disappointment and fear there and she just wanted to protect him from it all.

She just hoped that it wasn't too late yet.

Remember when it was said that cats could actually mimic the sounds they hear around them?

Well, they could actually mimic snake's hisses, too. They do this a lot of times when they do not like the people around them, when they feel threatened, and when they want to intimidate whoever is around them.

William Jarvis

Sometimes, they also do it when they're scared. Instead of showing the enemy that they are in fear, they'd just hiss as a means to protect themselves. They always want to be seen as creatures who are brave and strong—not the other way around.

More so, it's also a sign that they don't like what's happening and they'd rather be somewhere else—or they want their humans to be somewhere else. They also do this as a means to protect their friends, and their humans, but the thing is humans just see this as a form of aggression.

If only cats could talk, they probably would have told you how stupid you are and how uncanny you can be for not listening to them.

CHAPTER 6
SUSPICIOUS MOVES

"Here, have some chamomile tea," Audrina said as she placed a tray of tea on the table. "I heard that's great for trying to calm down or whatever." Troy, Emmy, and Daniel were all sitting on the couch, looks of fear on their faces.

"Look, that was unfortunate," Audrina said. "But, see? I guess we're right, Troy...maybe there's something suspicious about that Caleb guy. We don't know much about him; remember that's what I keep telling you?"

"So now this is my fault?" Troy argued. "His wife died, okay? Lay off him. I know we don't know everything about him but what's the point? What are you guys trying to prove here? If people were this way towards me when my wife died—"

"Dad, this isn't about his wife," Emmy said. "What did you say her wife's name was? Rose, right?"

"Yeah, why?"

"Well...I...I had a vision."

"What?" Both Troy and Daniel asked at the same time.

"What do you mean, Emmy?" Troy asked.

"In my mind, I heard that he was fighting with this woman named Marissa and they were fighting about a girl. And then Marissa said something about Caleb wanting to kill her and they kept on fighting and the next thing I knew, there was this loud explosion. I really couldn't explain it, dad, but—"

"You saw that all in your head?"

"Yeah."

"Well, maybe that means that you've just been so stressed out and you need some rest," Troy said. "I know you also had visions before and were able to help the police find out the truth about what happened to Ruby and Annabeth and all those things, but this is different, Em. We don't know what happened."

"So, you're just going to believe that it was all an accident? That this Caleb guy has no business with you, has no ulterior motives, and his wife died of suicide? Look, even Sara and the police know that it's not as simple as that because if it was, he wouldn't have been taken for questioning. You just have to open up your mind to that."

"Troy, you need to stop being so kind and naïve," Audrina said. "You almost lost your daughter because of that before."

"Audrina—"

"What did you say?" Troy said through gritted teeth.

Audrina took a deep breath. "I'm just saying, even Wendy knows that something is up with that guy. You know that cat. She's sweet. She loves you. You know what it means when cats become aggressive, right? It means they're scared and they know something wrong is about to happen. It means they hate the person or the animal they're trying to attack. I know she's just a cat but you love her, Troy, and she loves you, and I think you should think about what happened earlier."

"And connect it to the things that happened in the past?" He said. "I thought we were all trying to move on here?"

"Yes, Troy," Daniel said, "What we're only saying is that...you know, maybe you should also try to understand that sometimes, things that are happening today could also be connected to the past. And, she's right. Wendy's not like that with other people. Maybe, we should take that as a sign that—"

"That Caleb is an evil person?" Troy asked. "That poor old Troy is wrong yet again and he really shouldn't be in business anymore? I get it. You're all trying to make me feel bad because you're young and able and I'm just me. But just remember that I tried to help you all the best way I could. I tried to be the best man I could for this family and yet, no one seems to realize that because you're all so busy trying to save the world. What about my passions? What about the things I'd like to do?"

"In case you didn't realize, Troy," Audrina said, "No one's asking you to stop doing those things! No one's asking you not to pursue your dreams! We're all just trying to tell you to make sense of things, see some light, and realize that you don't know everything. Some things happen because there are psychopaths in this world and you have to be vigilant!"

"But you're attacking me when all I've done is love you! Did you even try to support me? Did you even try to make me feel like I'm doing the right thing?"

"Wow, so now this is my fault?!" Audrina scoffed, "In case you didn't know, Troy, the reason why this is happening is because we're all trying to protect you! But you're just so full of yourself some days, haven't you realized? I don't want to argue with you anymore. Let us all end up dead, if that's what you want!" She then made her way towards their room and slammed the door.

Troy took a deep breath as he faced Daniel and Emmy. "She's being preposterous."

"No, she's not," Emmy said. "You know she's not." Wendy then purled around her leg and she felt compelled to pick her up.

"So, you're going to say that Wendy really knows something? That you believe something is up with Caleb just because of her and of your vision?"

"Well, in case you've forgotten, Daddy, my visions allowed everyone to know that two of your old friends plotted hard against you. In case you've forgotten, I risked my life just to try to save your ass and what do I get now? You simply do not believe me. How else can I protect you when you don't want to accept my help? How else can I help you when you keep on treating me like I don't matter? If you don't want to listen to me, fine. But at least, listen to your wife. You already lost one and I'm afraid you might lose Audrina, too if you keep on being stubborn."

Emmy then took Daniel's hand so they could get out the door. She then looked back at Troy and spoke. "Oh, and dad," She said, "I hope you know that I care about you, but right now, I just wish I didn't."

Then she closed the door behind her father, overwhelmed with emotions at what just happened.

The Cat Who Smelled Murder #1

In case you didn't know, cats are also loyal creatures—but they show their loyalty in a different manner than dogs do.

Sometimes, though, they're already showing how loyal they are but people still see it as just a means to gain affection, or be naughty, the way they usually are.

Take, for instance, that cat who kept going back to his owner's house when he was left alone because his owners decided to move out. Or that cat who was rescued two weeks after the 9/11 attacks. He was found inside his owners' house who had to leave for a while because of the dust and fear as they were both at work that day, but weren't allowed to go home. The cat stayed in their house without eating for 2 weeks when he knew he could look for somewhere else to stay. He waited for his humans because of the belief that they'll still come back for him.

Most animals are that way. You may not realize it right away but once they know who their owners are, they will do everything they can to let their humans know that they love them. But as humans, we often fail to see that—because we only see them as manipulative little animals.

Cats love humans—they do. They just have no idea how to show it sometimes— just like the rest of us.

Chapter 7
Home, Let Me Go Home

"I couldn't believe him," Emmy said as she sat down on the couch with Wendy. They were back at home and she refused to speak all the way home. "I just couldn't believe him."

"You know how Troy can be, Em," Daniel said. "You've got to give him time."

"He's always just so trusting and he doesn't want to believe us. Sometimes, he's just so full of himself."

Just then, Bella made her way downstairs. "Hi," She said. "Charlize is asleep, but she might be awake in a bit...Uhm...how are you guys? Did your night go well?"

"So well I can't wait to go back there," Emmy answered sarcastically. "No, um...it was fine, Bella, thanks for asking. You can go home now. Dan, just—"

Dan reached into his pocket for his wallet and took out a few dollars. "Sorry, we got home late. Something just happened."

"About Caleb Roberts' wife?"

"How do you know that?" Emmy asked. "Do you know Caleb?"

Bella blushed. "No, um...I don't. I just heard it from a friend. I was worried. I'm glad you two were okay."

"Yeah, his wife died at home," Emmy said. "Police are saying that there was a suicide note, but we really don't know about that. You should go home now, Bella, it's late. I'll call your parents to apologize."

"No, don't!"

"Why not?"

"I mean," Bella took a deep breath, "They're away. They went with some of their friends to Cabo so I'm staying with one of my cousins for the weekend." She blushed some more and laughed awkwardly. "I really shouldn't be talking too much."

Wendy hissed and Daniel petted her to calm her down.

"I guess that's my cue, then." Bella smiled. "I'll see you guys around. Goodnight."

"Goodnight, Bella," Emmy said and they watched her walk out the door before going upstairs to check on their daughter.

Charlize's room had lavender walls with daisies painted on them. She was beautiful: she had Emmy's eyes and Daniel's lips, and for them, she looked like an angel. Emmy sure hoped that she'd grow up strong; that she'd know how to fend for herself in this uncanny world.

"She's beautiful," Daniel said, "just like you."

Emmy smiled at him. "She has your lips." She said as she picked Charlize up from her cot and carried her in her arms. "I wish I'm doing all I can as a mother."

"Hey," Daniel said, "You are. And one day, she'll be proud of you for all that you've done for this town, and for everything else that you could still do. She'll tell everyone about you, and remind you that the things you've done. The things you're going to do. They all matter."

Emmy took a deep breath as she prepared to breastfeed Charlize. "I hope you're right, Dan." She said. "I just…I hope that dad will be okay because even if I hate him right now, I still believe that we have to protect him. We're all he's got. I just…I have no idea what to do."

"Maybe, we could do what we've always done. What you've always done. Maybe, we have to figure out how this all started, and I guess your dream is a sign, Em." He said. "I'll make us some tea then see what's on TV. I'll just be downstairs."

"Dan," She said, as Daniel was making his way out of the room, "Thanks."

He smiled. "We're in this together, remember?"

She smiled back and hope sprung in her heart.

The Cat Who Smelled Murder #1

Cats know when their humans are in danger. In fact, even if they're not indoor cats, as long as they know someone takes care of them, they'll do all their best to make sure those people feel special and that they're able to give back, even in the smallest ways possible.

There's this cat named Tara who saved a boy named Jeremy from a neighbor's dog a couple of years ago. Jeremy was playing outside when a dog bit him, and the cat was there to pull the dog away from him, by means of scratching the said dog. It was a total David and Goliath match.

Jeremy's parents were surprised because Tara was used to staying outdoors and they didn't know that she would risk her life for Jeremy. Both Tara and Jeremy got stitches after what happened, but it let Tara's humans know that even if they're not around, Jeremy would be taken care of because she cared about him.

Then, there's also a cat named Mrs. Chippy who was once on an Antarctic Expedition. Mrs. Chippy was actually a he and was known for his ferocious but adorable spirit, and for the fact that he kept the ship's crew alive just by being around. Well, the crew and the ship met an accident and when worse came to worst, the Captain decided that Mrs. Chippy, along with the other animals on the ship have to be shot because they probably wouldn't survive and it would be hard for everybody to accommodate them anymore. Mrs. Chippy's owner was so mad at the Captain but didn't know what to do. Soon, when they all survived— minus Mrs. Chippy—a postage stamp was made for her but that, of course, wasn't enough because she was no longer around—even though she was one of the most loyal and friendly animals who ever graced this earth.

Funny how some humans show appreciation and gratitude, right?

CHAPTER 8
SUICIDE... OR NOT

"Thanks," Emmy said as Daniel handed her a cup of tea and they watched the news together. The reporter, Mary Elizabeth Johnson, was talking about what happened at the Byrnes' residence. Emmy also noticed that Wendy was on the couch, stirring in her sleep, probably dreaming again. She petted Wendy then turned her attention to the television.

"Rose Lyndon-Roberts died tonight due to unexplained circumstances. The police found a suicide note at the crime scene but are determined to take into consideration the fact that this might not really be the case. This stems from the fact that some neighbors said they often heard the couple arguing, and that before Caleb left the house earlier, he and his wife had another row."

Daniel sat down beside Emmy and saw the reporters interviewing Sara, who was now the Head Police Officer of the Sky Valley Jail.

"Yes, we found a suicide note but we're not convinced that it is the case. For one, the note was written on a piece of stationery and a glittery pen was used. It differs for everyone, yes, but if you come to think of it, someone on the brink of depression—someone who wants to kill herself—probably wouldn't think of using something so chic. But again, these are just speculations and we're still trying to find out the truth."

"Is it true that you took Mr. Roberts for questioning?"

"Yes," Sara answered, *"He has been cooperative, so far. That's all I can say."*

"Will we get to know the autopsy reports? When are you planning to do so?"

"You saw Mr. Roberts at The Byrnes' residence, right? Do you think this has something to do with what happened to Annabeth Meyer before? Do you think Emmy knows something about this?"

"This is a completely different case, but we're doing all that we can to see whether there actually are any connections, let's just leave it at that. We'll answer further questions soon."

The video went back to Mary Elizabeth Johnson. She spoke once more.

"In the history of Sky Valley, one can say that there's nothing more controversial than the murders that happened in the past year or two. From the murder of Annabeth Meyer in the once celebrated Time for Coffee, to the deaths of Ruby and Edward Scott, and to how Emmy Byrne, Troy Byrne's daughter, helped solve the seven-year-old crime involving the death of Lucy Watts, one can say that the past years have been eventful for the Byrnes—and for the rest of Sky Valley."

"You got to hand it to these reporters," Emmy said, "They string things fast, huh?"

Daniel tapped her on the knee and they watched some more.

"Tonight was supposed to be the launch of Troy Byrne's new business venture with Caleb Roberts. But with these recent developments, could Byrne's future be thwarted? Or, maybe it's just a sign that he's not supposed to do business anymore because the effects might be grim for everyone? We'll leave you with some words from Mr. Caleb Roberts himself, fresh from questioning. Good night, Sky Valley."

A clip of Caleb, all sweaty and nervous, was shown and Daniel and Emmy watched intently.

"I did not kill my wife. I know our relationship isn't perfect, but I would never in my wildest dreams think of killing her. I love her. That's all I'm ever going to say. You'll see, I didn't kill her. I would never do that."

Caleb was led to his car by another guy who was possibly his lawyer and then Wendy woke up and growled at the television. RAAAWWWRRRRRRR!

Daniel and Emmy looked at each other and as Emmy picked Wendy up, her mind spun in circles yet again and she heard words that she was sure Daniel didn't hear.

I hate you, Caleb! I hate you! You ruined our lives! You ruined me!

Rose, you have no idea what you're talking about! Just let me go. This is an important night.

How very clever. You couldn't even stay so we could sort out our problems?

That couldn't happen in just a night!

That would never happen at all! I can't believe I ever loved you!

"Em? Em? Are you okay?" Daniel asked, bringing Emmy back to the present. "What happened?"

Emmy looked Daniel in the eyes. "I think I should find out more about him, Dan." She said. "I think Caleb is hiding a lot of things from us and we have to figure it out before it's too late."

The Cat Who Smelled Murder #1

Another fascinating thing about cats?

They actually have the power to dream. When they're relaxed in their sleep, Rapid Eye Movement or REM also happens, the way it does for most people. This is because cats actually have the same brain patterns that people do; they have the capacity to think like humans, so they dream like humans, too.

That's exactly the reason why they act as if they know things that you don't. That's exactly why they act as if they understand you, and also why they could manipulate you, and make you run on their own accord. Needless to say, cats won't ever be outsmarted—and that's one thing you could be sure of.

Who knows?

Maybe one day, cats will take over the world—and all the dreams they have inside their heads would turn into reality.

CHAPTER 9
GETTING TO KNOW YOU

The sound of fingers typing was loud as Emmy tried to find out everything she could about Caleb Roberts. By googling his name, she was easily able to find out that he already lived in Georgia years ago, in Sky Valley, to be exact. His family was originally from Tallulah Falls but decided to move to Sky Valley when Caleb was in High School. He attended Sky Valley Private High and graduated Valedictorian, which also helped him earn early admission to Stanford University.

She even found a copy of his High School Valedictory Speech and tried so hard to keep Wendy at bay because she kept on putting her paws on the monitor, hissing like an enemy was around.

GRRRRRR WRRRRRRRR

"Wendy, please," Emmy said.

"Come now, Wendy," Daniel said while carrying Charlize. "Come on, let's eat outside." Daniel led Wendy downstairs so he could prepare some food for her.

Emmy went on to read Caleb's speech.

"Ladies and gentlemen, I'd like to thank each of you for being here. Most of you probably don't know me, but that doesn't matter. What really matters is that I'm here, thanks to the help of my parents, and my classmates are here also because of the help and support of their own families.

The road to success isn't smooth. I'm pretty sure it will only get harder from here on, but I hope that it won't be a reason for any of us to give up. If we've made it through the cruel world of High School, I'm sure we could move on to grander and better things.

And that's what matters, you know?

We all have to aim as high as we can, because only then will we be able to push ourselves to do what we have to do; to become the kind of people we're meant to be. And that's the kind of thing that I would like to leave with you all.

I want you all to remember that once upon a time, there was a boy who wondered how to be successful. And then, one day, that boy became a man and became everything he wanted to be. It's not wrong to be ambitious; in fact not having any ambitions at all is the worst thing you could do to yourself."

Emmy took a deep breath. She thought that Caleb truly was ambitious and that it seemed as if he had all these plans for his life, and it didn't really matter how he'd be able to pursue them. She searched some more and saw that he took up *Marketing Management* in college, graduated at the top of his class, and took up *Economic Analysis and Policy* in Graduate School. Afterward, he worked for some of the top brands in London and moved back to New York to start his own silverware business. The business flourished, but came to a point when some of his business partners betrayed him, so he lost a lot of money—all when he was 25, four years ago.

This prompted him to go back to Sky Valley, but it was unclear what he'd been doing then. The next thing Emmy found out was that he married one Marissa Hart, a beautiful, 25-year-old woman who was the Heiress to the Hart Publishing Industries fortune. Marissa was vacationing in Sky Valley with her parents when Caleb met her, and they hit it off right away. They got engaged in 2 weeks and were married soon after.

However, things came to a halt when after 2 years of being married, Marissa Hart died, due to a car accident—at least, that's what the police ruled it out to be. And Emmy didn't know how to feel about that because Lena McMahon was still the queen of the police force then. What was confusing though was that just nine months after Marissa died, Caleb married another woman, Rose Rivers, his wife who just died this evening.

Caleb said that he met Rose while working at this restaurant that he put up in Reynolds Square, where Rose's dad was an investor and that he found her to be caring and understanding in every possible way. Even though Marissa's parents disapproved of the union (because they thought it was too early for Caleb to marry someone else again), they couldn't do anything anymore and soon enough, Caleb and Rose were married. Emmy also learned that problems started to arise when Rose got pregnant and that she had two miscarriages. Rose never really wanted to give an interview about her situation, but being the daughter of one of the richest men in Georgia, she felt like she didn't have a choice. She also said that married life wasn't as easy as it seemed, but they're trying their best to make it work.

"Found anything?" Daniel asked as he came back into the room. "Wendy's eating downstairs."

Emmy took Charlize from him gently. "Yeah," she answered, "And you know…I think we have a case here." She said. "Caleb's the type of guy who keeps marrying women who are, well, richer than him. I think he wants to get into their pants because he wants a share of their riches, and obviously, he's not going to get any now because I don't think Rose made her will already."

"So, you're saying he's using these women to advance in his career?"

"That's more like it."

Daniel nodded his head. "What's your plan now?"

Emmy took a deep breath. "I'm going to attend his wife's funeral tomorrow. I'll see what I can find out."

And she sure hoped that she was going to do the right thing.

The Cat Who Smelled Murder #1

Do you know why cats sometimes act like people?

Aside from having the same brain waves, they also have the same emotional patterns. In fact, they can absorb a person's mood so easily that when you're sad, they'd probably be sad, too. They know how to be happy, they know how to be angry—and that's why cat owners are not crazy when they talk and interact with their pets.

But, did you also know that cats can heal you when you feel sad?

Of course, they wouldn't be able to solve your problems right away. No one will be able to do that. But, they'll be there for you in such a way that when they purr, and you pet them, they're able to deliver magnetic waves to the body that then calm the mind. Scientists still haven't been able to figure out how exactly cats purr, but they agree that purring is essential—and that even men could benefit from it.

Another thing?

Cats' brains are more similar to men's brains than to other animals. Forget about Planet of the Apes, soon, this world may be the Planet of the Cats.

Don't say I didn't warn you.

CHAPTER 10
THE CAT KNOWS

Meeeeoooow—meeeooooooow---prrrrrrrrr

"Wendy, Wendy where are you going?" Emmy asked as she saw Wendy going downstairs, all the way to a dark, rose-lined alley. She knows this place. She has been here a couple of times before, in her dreams.

"Wendy!"

Meooooowwwwwwwwrrrr

She followed Wendy and saw the well. The well was surrounded by roses and vines and there she saw Ruby and Annabeth, both beautiful, both looking radiant.

"Here you are again, Emmy," Annabeth said, still impatient and bossy even in death. "I thought we were over this. I thought you already knew what to do! And yet, here you are again, running in circles."

"Maybe, you shouldn't help them out anymore," Ruby said. "But then again...how would they get any help if you're not there."

"Do you girls know anything?" Emmy asked.

"Of course." Annabeth laughed. "Duh." She sighed and swooped her long white dress around Emmy. "You know the secret, right?"

"What do you mean? What secret?"

Annabeth sighed. "For someone so smart, you tend to be stupid sometimes, you know?" She went on. "The secret is what you've always known all along. Ambitions are deadly. Women are dangerous."

"Wait...what?"

"The cat knows," Ruby said. "She always knows. Right, Wendy?"

Emmy woke up from her reverie as she drank some more water. She was at the funeral of Rose Rivers-Roberts that evening and she remembered the dream she had last night. Whenever all this crazy stuff happen in Sky Valley, it seems like Ruby and Annabeth were there to help her. And based on her dream, it felt like Wendy knew a lot, too.

Everything was confusing, though. Apart from what she found out last night, Caleb actually looked pretty sad that his wife was gone—or maybe he was just a good actor. But then again, Emmy had a great feeling about these things. She knew when people were just acting, pretending to be who they're not. Caleb seemed to be sincere, though, but it was as if he was scared of some things, too. The look on his face signified not only sadness, but also fear—and Emmy was determined to find out what he's so scared of.

She was on the way back to the chapel where the wake was being held until she saw Caleb talking to a woman near the backyard. She looked around her and when she realized that no one else was around, she decided to eavesdrop and positioned herself near a pillar. She saw that the woman seemed a bit younger than Caleb (maybe two to three years younger), had brown locks, and was wearing a white, body-con lace dress.

"What else are you still waiting for?" She asked.

"I don't know, Ashley," Caleb replied. "But I don't want to be insensitive. We have to wait a while. I mean...these things aren't as simple as they seem, you know?"

"So, now you wouldn't want to be insensitive?" Ashley scoffed. "If you didn't want to be insensitive and if you really cared about your wife, you wouldn't have gotten together with me in the first place." She then placed her arms on Caleb's shoulders. "You love me, Caleb. You want me to be in your bed and in your life. Your wife's gone now. She killed herself. Or maybe, it's you who killed her, huh?"

"I would never do that."

"Really? Coz as for what I've heard, you also had something to do with your first wife, Marissa's death."

Caleb was dumbfounded. "Where did you hear that? That's not true."

"Whatever, Caleb, if you don't want to marry me, fine. But don't think that I'll hang around for long."

"Ashley, it's not like that."

"Whatever you say." She rolled her eyes and walked away from him.

Caleb kicked the curb and Emmy was surprised because he decided to go back inside, choosing the direction where Emmy was standing. They shared a look and then Caleb took a deep breath and went back inside.

The Cat Who Smelled Murder #1

*Once in the town of Hull in Yorkshire, there was a cat who was called "Sparky."
Sparky's name was originally Soxy, but he was christened anew when he went to
an electric field in Hull and was electrocuted with 11,000 Bolts of Electricity.*

*Sparky didn't die, though, but he suffered. For a while, his face and body were
burned and his legs were paralyzed but his owners recognized him and promised
to take care of him even more. The community thought of him as a superhero,
and for a time, he became popular and was the subject of many stories.*

*But the thing is that one day, Sparky was able to escape out of his humans'
house again, went back to the electric field, and this time, wasn't able to survive.*

You know what it means, though?

*I guess that's a big sign that people, more often than not, refuse to learn from
their mistakes. Most people are stubborn, and sometimes that leads them—and
those around them—to a lot of danger.*

CHAPTER 11
YOU WOULDN'T BELIEVE WHAT I SAW

"So, you saw him talking to this woman named Ashley and then?" Daniel asked Emmy, who was now carrying Charlize in her arms. They were in the living room and Emmy was trying to recall what she saw earlier.

"Well, they were obviously in a heated conversation and Ashley was saying that because Rose is now dead, Caleb has to marry her. I think they're already in a relationship."

"He was cheating on Rose?"

"Yeah," Emmy said, "and I think he promised Ashley that he would marry her, or at least, that's what she thinks. They were arguing, Dan, and he was like, I didn't kill Rose, and then she blurted out something about how he killed his first wife. Remember my visions? I'm not sure if it was a car accident or something but it felt like Ashley was convinced that it wasn't an accident, and she was so adamant about telling him that she wants to get married or else, she wouldn't be with him anymore."

"Whoa," Daniel said.

"I know," Emmy muttered and sighed. "And it doesn't help that I've been having these dreams about Ruby and Annabeth and how they're saying that the woman is evil, that the woman is the problem...I don't know if they're right or—"

"What is your intuition telling you?"

Meewwwww Meewwwwwwww Wendy was meowing and making hissing sounds again, but Daniel and Emmy were too preoccupied with their conversation that they didn't really mind her right away.

"I don't know, Dan." She said. "I mean, this isn't an easy thing and I can't just make conclusions. Wait—" She then took out her phone and made a Google Query about *"Caleb Roberts and Ashley"*.

Almost no results came up, except for a photo taken from an article in the Sky Valley Daily. Emmy clicked it open and read.

Late last night, Caleb Roberts, the husband of Rose Rivers-Roberts of the Sky Surprise Restaurant Chain, was seen with a brunette woman near Reynolds Square. Sources say that the woman, only known as "Ashley", has been seen with Roberts on a couple of occasions when his wife was away with her family.

Could this be the start of the fallout of their relationship?

If you may recall, Caleb Roberts was once married to Publishing Heiress Marissa Hart before she died in a tragic accident. Could it be that once again, Roberts has found someone else? Could this be karma for Rose Rivers already?

"That was harsh," Daniel said. "Who wrote that?"

"Some showbiz reporter," Emmy answered. "You know how they could be. Remember when they attacked us for Ruby's death, saying I was this whore and you didn't have a backbone and all?"

"Yeah, they could be nasty."

GRRRRROOOOOWWWWLLL PRRRRRRRRR

Once again, Wendy made loud sounds and Emmy and Dan couldn't ignore her anymore because she kept on going back and forth to the door leading to the backyard.

"What's wrong with her?" Emmy asked.

"I don't know," Daniel said, "she's been like that ever since I came home.'

"Have you checked the backyard?"

"No, not really," Daniel said. "I thought she was just having some of her jealousy attacks because I was with Charlize earlier."

"Come on," Emmy said and followed Wendy towards the door.

MEWWWW MEWWWWWWWWW

Daniel opened the door as he carried Charlize and Emmy followed Wendy towards one of the trees. She then saw that just by the foot of the tree was a box tied with a red ribbon.

"What the hell is that?" Daniel asked. "Don't—"

But before he could finish what he was about to say, Emmy already opened the box and was shocked at what she saw.

Inside the box lay a bloody baby doll and with it came a note. Emmy took the note with trembling hands as the doll fell on the floor and read:

Can't stop poking your head into everything, huh?

Well, do that some more and next time, you and your child may be in this box.

Don't think that this is a threat; take it as a warning.

Emmy and Daniel looked at each other and all Emmy could think of was how Caleb saw her after his conversation with Ashley earlier.

The Cat Who Smelled Murder #1

You may also never find animals with such willpower as cats.

Take for example Scarlett, this cat who was deemed as an action hero. No, she wasn't in any action films, wasn't bungee jumping, or jumping off heights and all that, but she was the kind of cat who was brave enough to rescue her kittens from raging fire, even though she was burned herself. She survived, though, and her story has inspired millions all over the world.

And then there's Bart, more popularly known as the Zombie Cat. He once got himself into a traffic accident, was accidentally buried alive, and right out of a movie, was able to make his way out of the grave simply by using his claws!

You see, cats aren't only jealous, manipulative, domineering creatures—they could also remind you that life is precious and they'd do everything they can to save themselves and save the ones they love.

I guess people should take a cue from that instead of acting high and mighty all the time and thinking that they can survive life all on their own, without the littlest amount of help whatsoever.

CHAPTER 12
EVERYONE'S DANGEROUS

Meeeeow Meeewwww Prrrrrrr Purrrrrrr Sssssss

"Wendy, it's late, we could no longer go out."

Mewwwwwww

Emmy looked at her and found everything to be cloudy and hazy like she really wasn't at home anymore. Once again, she was back in the world of her dreams; a world that helped her out before but she wasn't sure was working now.

Meeeeeeew

"Wendy! Let's go home!" But Emmy still followed Wendy, who was now making her way towards Ruby.

"Ruby, give her back."

"Why don't you listen to the signs around you, Emilia?" She asked. "Would you rather let your cat die? Would you rather let your daughter die?"

"What are you talking about?"

"You are just like your father. Look at the well."

Emmy was confused but did as she was told. When she looked into the well, she saw Caleb—he was definitely younger, more confident but had that look of anger on his face. He was talking to a woman, but Emmy couldn't see the woman's face. She only heard them speak.

"You're not going to that convention, you freak!"

The Cat Who Smelled Murder #1

"What did you just say?"

"Are you even married to me, huh? Or did you just use me so you could get back on track, use all my assets and you'd rather just throw me away afterward?"

"You're being paranoid."

"And you're being stupid. Don't think that I'm not a smart person, Caleb. I know what you're doing. I know what you're trying to do."

"You know what? Fine. If you don't trust me, get in the car with me. Come to the convention with me. God knows you can use a little bit of time outside as all these time you spend at home is fucking with your brains!"

"Fuck you!"

"You heard that, Emmy? You see how they fought? But, of course, that's just the tip of the iceberg, right, Wendy?" Wendy purred.

"Give me Wendy back."

"No, this isn't over yet." It was now Annabeth's turn to speak. She looked radiant like she never died at all. In fact, she looked like she was at her best. "Look into the well again, Emmy."

"Why are you even doing this?"

"Because you need us, duh!" Annabeth said. "Just look into the well, please."

Emmy did as she was told and noticed how the well turned into a blurry puddle of mud—or whatever it was. And then flowers bloomed and died and another vision was being shown straight to her.

This time, it was of Caleb and Rose fighting.

William Jarvis

"I'm tired, Rose, lay off me, please."

"You're tired?" Rose said, crying. In this dream, her face was scary, botched like she was really dead and something terribly wrong happened to her. "You're tired, Caleb? Well, what about me? I spend all day trying to beautify the house for you, cooking the best meals for you...I've even forgotten about my own life already! I've given up all of my friends for you and what do I get out of this? Nothing! You go out there, do what you want, use all of my money—"

"Your money?! I worked hard for what I have, too!"

"But you needed my help, Caleb! You needed my help, and you know that! We both know you only didn't marry me because you loved me! You also needed my money! You think I don't hear the news? You think I don't know about you and this Ashley girl? Don't underestimate me, Caleb."

"You're just tired."

"Yeah, I am. I'm tired of everything. I'm tired of being alone, mourning for kids that would never grow up because my body's not strong enough for them. I'm tired of being around you and feeling like...like I don't know who you are anymore." She was crying now, crying so hard that Emmy felt bad for her. "I'm tired of feeling like I'll be dead anytime soon. You know, maybe they're right when they said that you had something to do with Marissa's death. Maybe, this really is karma biting me in the butt."

"You don't know that. And you know what? You just have to relax. I'm tired of all this fighting!"

Emmy heard some punches being thrown and she wasn't sure who did that. She looked at Annabeth and Ruby. "What was that about? Are you telling me that Caleb really had something to do with his wife's death?"

"I think you already know the answer," Ruby said as Wendy purred. "Wendy does."

"I don't think Emmy knows," Annabeth said. She looked Emmy in the eyes. "But I think you know what lesson you've learned in the past year or so. I mean, you've learned a lot, but there's one thing, one big thing that encompasses it all, right?"

Emmy took a deep breath and took Wendy and placed her on her lap. "Yeah," She muttered, "That I really couldn't trust anyone. Everyone's dangerous."

"You bet they are," Annabeth said. "So you have to be extra careful. Especially now."

William Jarvis

You know how great cats' detective skills are?

Well, you could take into consideration Fred, also known as the Undercover Kitty, who helped out the Brooklyn Attorney's Office in 2006 as a bait to figure out whether one Steven Vassar was a real veterinarian or not. Fred was able to solve the case, and with his wit—he was named after Fred Weasley of the Harry Potter Series—was applauded by everyone.

He was undergoing training as a therapy cat, you know, one of those cats who massage adults and children alike to help heal their afflictions, and became part of a couple of programs and events hosted by the NYPD. He received numerous awards and distinctions and even had offers to appear in commercials and movies.

Sadly, his life was cut short when he escaped from the home of the people who adopted him, and was struck by a car, killing him right away.

Maybe, that's really the thing about life. The good ones just go away a little too soon—and you have to give them all you've got, all your life because you never really know when they could be taken away from you. After all, everything is on borrowed time—and people forget that a little too often.

CHAPTER 13
BLOODY DOLL

"This is…creepy," Sara said as Emmy showed her the bloody doll that she found last night at home. Emmy still hated being in the police station because it reminded her of Lena McMahon and of all the things that happened before. She also couldn't stand the fact that Bree and Laurel were there, and somehow, she felt bad because she never really wanted to put anyone in jail, especially people who were only confused and didn't realize the crimes they committed. But that's life: you just have to be strong through it all.

"So," Sara continued, "you just found this in your backyard?"

"Yeah, last night. Wendy, my cat, she led us there." Emmy explained. "I didn't really know what to expect and when I opened the box, that was there. And, of course, there's the note."

Sara took the note from the box and read it out loud.

Can't stop poking your head into everything, huh?

Well, do that some more and next time, you and your child may be in this box.

Don't think that this is a threat; take it as a warning.

Sara took a deep breath. "Have you had any problems with anyone recently? I mean, have you gotten into some arguments and the like?"

"No, not really," Emmy said. "Except for my father, but I'm pretty sure he wouldn't do that. He's just upset that we warned him about Caleb and you know what happened there. And speaking of Caleb…" Emmy took a deep breath.

"What is it, Em?"

"Well, I saw him talking to a woman the other night. You know, at Rose's wake. The woman's name was Ashley and they were arguing. I think they're in a relationship."

"Is this the same Ashley who was in that newspaper article, about Caleb possibly cheating on Rose or something?" Sara asked.

"Yeah, that's the one," Emmy answered. "They were arguing hard last night and she was like, they should get married right away since Rose is already dead. I've also learned that Caleb has this habit of marrying women who are more financially able than him. And I got another dream about that last night, about how Caleb and Rose argued over money and miscarriages."

"Wow," Sara said. "I mean, we looked into that the other night and we also figured that out. It's like, he's using these women as a means to get back on track, be successful again, especially after his failures at 25...thanks for the information, Em."

"Yeah, and another thing," She said, "Caleb saw me. He...he knew I was listening to them. But I really don't know if it was him who sent the doll because when I saw him last night, he looked really harassed like he also didn't like what was happening. I mean, I'm not sure about anything right now, Sara, but I don't think we should make extreme conclusions, but we should look at each and every possible angle."

"Yes, we're doing that," Sara said. "Caleb also told us that although he doesn't deny fighting with his wife the night that she died, he didn't kill her and he wouldn't think of doing that in a million years. Everyone says that, of course, but somehow...I felt like in a way, he was sincere, you know what I mean? The only thing that bothers me is that he never admitted that he's in a relationship with Ashley."

"Who would ever admit that they're cheating on their wife?" Emmy asked. "I'm pretty sure he'll find a way to announce their relationship to the world soon. Anyway," she said, "I need to be somewhere for now."

"Where are you going? Do you want one of the men to go with you? I can totally arrange for that."

"No, no, don't bother." She said. "It's okay, Sara. Don't worry about me. I have a plan."

William Jarvis

Did you know that there was once a Maine Coon who ran in the Senatorial Race?

Yep, it really happened.

Just like Emmy's cat Wendy, Hank was also a Maine Coon, who lived in Virginia. In the US Political Elections of 2012, he was put up for election by his owners named Anthony Roberts and Matthew O'Leary, because they were fed up with the state of politics in America.

As a result, they created a website for Hank, a biography, and were even able to collect around $16,000 of donations meant for the campaign and for Hank's platform of "Positive Campaigns, Spay and Neuter Programs, and Animal Rescue and Welfare." Hank only ranked third in the race, but at least, because of the love and support people bestowed upon him, a lot of animals' lives were saved.

But just imagine if Hank could talk and really put his heart and mind to the campaign! I'm pretty sure it would be a big change in the political arena and for the whole state of the world, you know?

CHAPTER 14
YOU KNOW WHAT TO DO

Emmy was standing near the Sky Cornerstone, another restaurant that was a big part of her past, especially because Angeline died there and they were also able to solve that case. She didn't really plan on going there today, but she felt like she needed some air and the Cornerstone had a really nice Al-Fresco dining option, so she bought herself a tall glass of Mango Shake and sat down so she could try to calm herself.

Her plan didn't go so well.

She went to Cassiopeia's house to ask her for help. Cassiopeia is Audrina's friend who was also psychic. Cassiopeia was instrumental in the solving of Lucy's case, and that's why Emmy thought that she might be able to help them out, too. But, when she arrived at her place, she noticed that Cassiopeia's purple house was closed and she saw a signage on the door that said that Cassiopeia was on vacation and she would be back next month.

Of course, Emmy knew that she could no longer wait for the following month, especially in a situation like this, but she didn't really know what to do about that. Sometimes, she wished she also could just go somewhere far and forget about everything for a while, but she knew that she couldn't do it right now, because she had Charlize, and Wendy, and there was this case. And, besides, she also felt like she didn't want to leave her family alone, even if she and her father were not in good terms right now.

"Honey, none of this is your fault," Daniel said. He was currently at work right now and Charlize was home with Bella. "I mean, you didn't know Cassiopeia wouldn't be there. And this isn't even your job to begin with. I know you're trying your best to help but don't let this get the best of you."

"Yeah, but...I don't know. I just thought things would be easier."

"Do you want me to pick you up? I can ask for a day off."

"No, Dan. It's fine. Don't interrupt your schedule for this." Just then Emmy saw someone waving at her: it was Libby, one of Lucy's old friends. They kept in touch a bit after what happened and then she heard that Libby went to Vegas. But apparently, she's back now. "Wait, I'll see you later, okay? Libby's here."

"Libby? Great! Give her my regards."

"Will do. I love you."

"I love you, too."

"Oh my god, Em!" Libby greeted as she came up towards Emmy when she saw Emmy put down her phone. She gave Emmy a hug and bussed her on the cheek. "I missed you so much! I'm glad to see you!"

"Glad to see you, too." Emmy smiled and held Libby's hand. "It's been a while! I heard you were in Vegas?"

"Yeah, for a while," Libby said. "I wanted to travel a bit. I'm just here for a vacation, actually, then I'll be back in school. I'm taking up Fashion Design now. Maybe I could intern for you one day?"

"That sounds like a great idea." She smiled.

"But you don't seem like you're okay. How are you?"

"Yeah...uhn...things have been complicated." Emmy then told her about Caleb Roberts and everything she's learned about him and about the doll that she found at home. By the end of it, Emmy felt herself being nervous and frustrated, especially after she told Libby about her plan of asking Cassiopeia for help and finding out that she actually wasn't around.

"I see," Libby muttered and took a deep breath. "I'm really sorry about this. That doll was seriously creepy, I feel like Caleb has something to do with it. I remember him being in school, you know? He was seriously smart and was popular so even though we weren't from the same batch, I knew about him. He's smart but seriously ambitious and...and he always had this creepy factor about him. Also, when he came back here to marry Marissa Hart, I don't think anyone really approved, the way he wanted them to. My parents knew Marissa's parents as they all went to school together and they thought that everything happened too fast, but they couldn't tell Marissa that they didn't want her to marry Caleb because well, she's their only daughter and they wanted her to be happy. You know the deal."

"What about Rose? Do you know anything about her?"

"No, not really. I don't think her family's originally from here, although they became extremely successful because of their restaurants. Hey, wait," Libby said, "I have an idea."

"What do you mean?"

"Why don't we call Cassiopeia? Last I checked, she was in Hawaii. I'm pretty sure she wouldn't mind helping you."

"Oh, no, Libby, don't do that. I mean, she's on a vacation—"

"Don't be silly," Libby said. "I'm sure she'd be more than willing to help." She said. "Besides...this is the least I could do. You've done a lot for us in the past, you know?"

"Libs—"

But before Libby could say another word, Libby was already dialing Cassiopeia's number and was relaying the information that Emmy gave her. She then passed the phone to Emmy.

"Cassiopeia...hey, I'm really sorry...I just thought—"

"Libby told me everything," Cassiopeia said in her usual calming voice. "I'm sorry I'm not there right now, but I'll do the best I could, okay? For now, all I can tell you is that you really shouldn't trust the people you think are trustworthy...I'm sure you already know that. And...and you have to beware of another girl, a girl connected to this Caleb person."

"A...girl...you mean, Ashley?"

"I think so, yes," Cassiopeia said. "Also, it would help if you'd get to see Caleb."

"See him? As in meet up with him?"

"Yes. There are some things he wants to tell you, but couldn't tell you because he's scared. You have to be very careful. You know how to do this, Emmy. Just...be safe. It would also be better if you could bring your cat with you."

"My cat? As in, Wendy?"

"Yes, her," Cassiopeia answered. "She would help you out in terms of seeing the light, she'll shed some light over a lot of things."

"She hates Caleb."

"Just bring her with you. And don't worry, I'll try to be back as soon as I can, okay?"

"No, Cass, please enjoy your vacation. And thank you so much. You have no idea how much this could help."

"You be safe, okay? And don't worry, your father will come around soon."

Emmy couldn't help but smile lightly. "Thanks. Thanks a lot."

She handed the phone back to Libby. "I couldn't thank you enough, Libs."

"Don't worry, it's okay." Libby held her hand. "And I have complete faith in you. You'll figure this out. Do you want me to come with you? I can totally do that."

"No, don't bother, Libs. I'll be okay. I'll take it from here."

"Okay," Libby said. "Just remember, we're here for you, okay? Everything's going to be fine."

"Thanks, Libs."

And at that moment, Emmy felt like she really wasn't alone in this and that maybe, there was still hope, and everything would be better.

William Jarvis

Cats' claws could be dangerous—and scary, especially for some, but people still have no right to cut them.

The reason why it's wrong to do that is because doing so could be similar to cutting men's fingers from their knuckles. A cat has claws so he can protect himself from enemies.

Keep in mind that not all cats live indoors. There are feral cats who have to be as brave as they can in the outside world, and without their claws, they wouldn't be able to fend for themselves in times of trouble. Humans are not always around— and not all of them are kind to cats.

So, just because you're used to trimming your nails doesn't mean that you can decide to cut a cat's nails, too. Just imagine how you'd feel without your fingers! You certainly wouldn't like that, would you?

CHAPTER 15
WE HAVE A LOT TO TALK ABOUT

Emmy walked out of her car with Wendy in hand. She was now standing outside *Byrne-Roberts Enterprise*, his father's flagship store with Caleb for their silverware. She knew that cats weren't really allowed there, but she couldn't just leave Wendy at home, especially after what Cassiopeia said.

Daniel also wanted to come with her, but she told him not to because she'd feel better knowing Daniel was with Charlize at home. After all, they really couldn't leave Charlize with Bella all the time as Bella also has a life of her own. And besides, she could always tell the people that she's Troy Byrne's daughter. The thing with small towns and popular people is that once you've made your mark, you have already made your mark—and people will almost always remember you. And Emmy hoped that today, it would come in handy.

Just before she walked towards the entrance, she felt dizzy and had another vision in her head. It wasn't as clear as the other visions she had in the past, but she swore she heard both Marissa and Rose's voices. They were both asking for help, wanting some clarity.

And then Ruby and Annabeth's advice rang in her ears.

"For someone so smart, you tend to be stupid sometimes, you know?" She went on. "The secret is what you've always known all along. Ambitions are deadly. Women are dangerous."

"Wait...what?"

"The cat knows," Ruby said. *"She always knows. Right, Wendy?"*

"You heard that, Emmy? You see how they fought? But, of course, that's just the tip of the iceberg, right, Wendy?"

"I think you already know the answer," Ruby said as Wendy purred. "Wendy does."

"I don't think Emmy knows," Annabeth said. She looked Emmy in the eyes. "But I think you know what lesson you've learned in the past year or so. I mean, you've learned a lot, but there's one thing, one big thing that encompasses it all, right?"

"You have to be extra careful. Especially now."

She shook her head and walked to the entrance with Wendy. Good thing that one of the guards, who've already worked with them before, recognized her and let her in. She told the receptionist that she wanted to talk to Caleb about business and because she also knew her, she let Emmy in.

"Amelia, I told you—"

"It's Emilia, but hello," Emmy said with a smile and saw the look of surprise on Caleb's face when she came in. He thought that it was the receptionist who came in and didn't really know what Emmy was doing there.

"Emmy," Caleb said. "What are you doing here? And you have Wendy with you—"

"Yeah, well, don't worry, she's calm now. Right, baby?"

Wendy hissed at Caleb and just purled around Emmy's leg.

"Is there anything I can do for you?"

"Oh, we just have a lot to talk about, actually."

Caleb gave her a look of confusion. "What do you mean?"

"Didn't you just send me a bloody doll last night? A doll that's full of blood with a note that says that I should shut my mouth and stop poking my head into things or I'll be next. Such a clever way of threatening me when we both know that you think I heard whatever it is that you and that Ashley girl were talking about. Or is there something you should be scared of, Caleb?"

"I—I don't know what you're talking about," Caleb said. "Why are you even here?"

"Really? You don't know what I'm talking about? What do you know, then?" Emmy asked and went on. "Oh, wait. I think you know something about how to hurt a woman...just like what happened to your first wife, Marissa, two years ago."

Caleb looked at her, dumbstruck. She knows that look—it was the look of someone who wanted to be anywhere but there.

William Jarvis

Almost every part of a cat's body is essential to his overall wellbeing.

His whiskers, for example, can measure directions. That's why some people who don't care for cats and want cats to be gone simply cut off the cats' whiskers so they'd be lost—and that's one of the worst things that one can do.

How a cat's whiskers work in helping him know where he's going is due to the fact that the whiskers are able to detect even the smallest changes in air pressure. So, when one cat is no longer in his house, or no longer in an area where he feels safe or one that is unfamiliar to him, he'll know it right away.

Without those whiskers, a cat won't be able to go home. So don't think of pulling them, cutting them, or ruining them in any way even if they're already long. Remember that just like people, cats have the right to find their way home, too.

CHAPTER 16
DYING IN HIS ARMS

(2 Years Ago)

It was a cold dark night and Marissa Hart-Roberts was again, not in a good mood. She felt ugly, inside and out. She had some breakouts, her hair was dry, her heart was heavy. Once again, her husband was about to go to another convention, another meeting, and for her, this was just a way of Caleb not to be around her.

She wasn't dumb. She knew that things have changed and that Caleb didn't love her the same way anymore. Even Caleb knew this himself.

If he had a choice, he wouldn't be with Marissa anymore but he didn't know how to tell her that. He didn't know how he'd be able to break up with her, and if he was being honest with himself, he wanted to be sure before he'd do it. He didn't want to get out of this marriage without anything. Of course, it was wrong to marry someone for their money but he needed to help himself. His parents were content with their average life and he didn't really want that. He always wanted more, more, more.

But Marissa wouldn't let him have that. She was, in his own opinion, very clingy. She was the perfect housewife, yes, but she wasn't the perfect wife—if there was any difference. She was just not her own person anymore. She and Caleb just kept on fighting and he was getting tired of it. And he has his eye on someone else now, you know? Rose Rivers. She seemed nice. She was rich. She'll help him out.

"You're not going to that convention, you freak!"

"What did you just say?"

William Jarvis

"Are you even married to me, huh? Or did you just use me so you could get back on track, use all my assets and you'd rather just throw me away afterward?"

"You're being paranoid."

"And you're being stupid. Don't think that I'm not a smart person, Caleb. I know what you're doing. I know what you're trying to do."

"You know what? Fine. If you don't trust me, get in the car with me. Come to the convention with me. God knows you can use a little bit of time outside as all these time you spend at home is fucking with your brains!"

"Fuck you!"

"Fuck you, too!"

"You know? Let me do just that. Let me come with you. Let's see what happens. You're nothing without me, anyway."

"Fine. I'm going now. Dress up if you want to!"

Marissa didn't dress up. She just went and followed Caleb all the way to his car. Little did Caleb know that it would be the last time they'd be riding that car together. It was the last time he'll ever get to talk to Marissa, argue with her, make her cry.

"Caleb, I love you. I love you so much my heart is going to break. You just have no idea, do you?"

"Why don't you just shut up? It was Caleb's voice, and he was so angry, so angry that Emmy felt his anger seethe towards hers; like it was so real; so raw."

"Shut up already."

"But what were you doing with her? Why were you calling her?"

"That's none of your business, Marissa. We work together. That's that."

"Yeah? But why do you often go out together? Why can't you leave each other alone?"

"You're insane. Back off, or something will happen."

"No, Caleb—"

"Marissa, stop—"

"I will not stop! I haven't been with you in a while and whenever we're together, you're acting like you just want to be somewhere else! You want me to be...be this person whom I'm not—"

"No, Marissa, you're turning me into the person I don't want to be with!"

"What the hell does that mean?!"

"It means what it means!"

"Are you going to kill me?!"

"Marissa, stop!"

"No, you stop! You're not going to do this!"

"Marissa!" There was an evident fear in his voice; fear mixed with anger; fear that could kill.

"Caleb, stop!!!!"

"Marissa!!!"

Caleb remembered everything about that night. He wanted to forget, but he couldn't. He remembered how they fought over the steering wheel. She remembered how Marissa tried to punch her, how she was so mad at him, how she felt that he wasn't being totally honest with her.

Her hands were on his. His body felt like it was going to separate from this moment, like he didn't want to be there anymore. He felt a lot of pain in his head while Marissa was screaming so hard for her life.

"I'm going to die! I'm going to die! You're killing me! I'm going to die!"

He didn't know if it was his fault. He didn't want to be at fault.

What about his plans?

What about everything he's worked hard for too long?

What about wanting to get back on top and be the best version of himself that he could be? What about showing everyone that they were wrong about him? That he could once again be rich, successful, and the envy of many?

What about all those things?

"CALEB!!!!!!"

His name was the last thing she ever uttered.

His name was on her lips while he died, little by little, in his arms.

It was one of the worst nights of his life because even if he wanted to end things with Marissa, he didn't want to end them that way. But nothing could be done about it anymore. What's happened already happened.

The Cat Who Smelled Murder #1

There was a flash of blinding light. There was a terrible collision. He came out of it unscathed, only with a few wounds and bruises and almost some broken bones, but the other car hit Marissa so bad—so bad, that she died right away.

And people blamed him for it. Maybe, they had every right to.

After all, if he was being honest with himself, he also wanted it to happen. He wanted her gone. But not in that way. Never in that way.

William Jarvis

Cats could be excellent guards, too.

Don't believe me?

Well, you could take the case of Mike, for example.

Mike used to guard the British Museum, one of the most famous and important museums in the world! And he learned all that he knew from the Museum's house cat, who from the time he was a kitten already taught him how to hunt birds and find his own food. Soon enough, Mike was already guarding the entrance to the museum and he did this for around twenty years!

Mike wasn't the type of cat who was friendly to everyone and that's why he was an excellent guard. He was the type of cat who knew that not all people are trustworthy. In fact, he would only allow specific people to feed him, and would growl and hiss so bad when he felt threatened and was especially close to the human guard of the museum. He knew that you didn't have to be friends with everyone and you only needed the best ones at hand.

When he died, TIME Magazine covered his death and his humans made obituaries about him. Needless to say, there was no other cat like Mike to guard the British Museum anymore. Many have tried, but no one was able to mimic Mike.

He left a legacy—and that legacy would forever remain untarnished.

CHAPTER 17
IT'S NOT WHAT YOU THINK

(Present Day)

Emmy saw that Caleb looked scared; that there was something terrible in his mind and that if he had a choice, he'd kick Emmy away right then and there.

"What is it, Caleb?" Emmy asked. "Thinking about how you killed your wife, huh?"

"It was an accident!" He said through gritted teeth. "I promise you it's not what you think. And besides, why do you even care? You didn't know Marissa."

"Maybe, I didn't." She said. "But I know my father. He's so trusting, and that's why he put his complete faith in you, to the point that he no longer cared that we were so worried about him. We had an argument, you know? When the police came for you, we told him that maybe, he really shouldn't be trusting you like that, but he argued with us. He's on your side, Caleb! And I don't want him to be wrong. So, it would be best if you could enlighten me now or I could call the police and tell them to question you more until you get so tired of all the questions already."

"Like I said," Caleb took a deep breath, "it was an accident. Marissa and I were fighting a lot but that...that wasn't enough for me to want to kill her."

"What were you fighting about?"

"Things." He said as he drank some water. "We didn't see eye to eye anymore. When you get married at an early age—"

"25 isn't really early. You shouldn't have married her if you weren't ready."

"I know." He said. "But I thought that she was nice, you know, and she could help me out. I know it sounds selfish to you, and maybe it really is, but you couldn't call me out on that. We do everything we can to survive in this world and sometimes, you have to rely on other people, ask them for help."

"You married her. You made her believe you were in love with her."

"I did. I did love her...maybe, just not in the way she deserved but I did. I was just...I had other things in mind."

"You were extremely ambitious," Emmy said. "I bet you still are."

"And aren't you? You went to Paris, right? You left your father when he needed you. I did my research, you know? Yeah, sure, you tried to make up for it by coming back here and saving everyone's lives but you know you're not perfect, Emilia. You had your faults, too. Why don't you just go home and take care of your daughter? That's where you belong."

Emmy laughed. "You're funny." She said. "You know what the problem with you is? You think you're so much better than everyone that you fail to realize that you have your own weaknesses, too. I'm doing what I can to save my family from people like you. My father is a part of my family, too. And you're right. Maybe, I did leave him before but unlike you, I didn't do it for selfish reasons. I was hurting, too. And now I'm trying all my best to make sure you don't ruin him."

"I'm trying to help him out."

"By not telling him everything about you? You can't help him out like that, Caleb. You have a hidden agenda. You can't marry my father, of course, but you're making your way into our lives because you know that he's rich and trusting and you now have another business under your name. But your wife's dead. Caleb. And you know what I think?"

Caleb looked at her before she spoke again.

"I think you have something to do with this, or Wendy wouldn't have clawed you like that."

William Jarvis

There's a cat who knows how to predict death.

This cat's name is Oscar and he's a resident therapy cat at the Steere House Rehabilitation and Nursing Center in Providence. Oscar was able to predict around twenty-five correct deaths.

The nurses know that the patients are dying whenever Oscar curls up with them on the bed. After a couple of hours, the said patients would be breathing their last breath.

No, Oscar's not the problem. He never killed and would never kill anyone. Doctors say that the reason why Oscar knows how to predict death is because when patients can no longer move properly, their bodies release a lot of ketones. Ketones are the biochemicals that are released by a dying person's body. It's also the same way mother cats know their kittens are dying. It's the same way cats know that they themselves are dying and that's why they choose to move somewhere else and go far from their humans. Cats really do not want their pet parents to know that they're on the brink of death.

Because of his death predictions, Oscar became popular as the cat who isn't friendly to the living. But, of course, if Oscar could speak, he'd say that this isn't true.

Oscar's ability is innate to him, just like some people's talents are to them. And it would be unfair to fault him for it. When you're dying, you're dying—it's as simple as that.

At least Oscar knows how to prepare you for it. Sometimes, it's better to be prepared than not know anything about what's going to happen next, right?

CHAPTER 18
A ROSE ISN'T ALWAYS A ROSE

"So now you're accusing me of being a serial wife killer, is that it?"

"That's a creative name. And you know what? I think that even if you didn't kill her, you led her to her death."

"I didn't kill her." He stated while looking her in the eye. "Think what you want to think but I didn't kill her. And besides, she's not the Rose that you think. Rose had her own faults, too, and she knew...she knew from the beginning that it wasn't all just about the love for us. She knew. But I loved her."

Emmy felt like Caleb was about to cry because of the strain in his voice; a strain that couldn't be denied. And then Emmy remembered her dream about Rose; about how she and Caleb argued.

"I'm tired, Rose, lay off me, please."

"You're tired?" Rose said, crying. In this dream, her face was scary, botched like she was really dead and something terribly wrong happened to her. "You're tired, Caleb? Well, what about me? I spend all day trying to beautify the house for you, cooking the best meals for you...I've even forgotten about my own life already! I've given up all of my friends for you and what do I get out of this? Nothing! You go out there, do what you want, use all of my money—"

"Your money?! I worked hard for what I have, too!"

"But you needed my help, Caleb! You needed my help, and you know that! We both know you didn't marry me only because you loved me! You also needed my money! You think I don't hear the news? You think I don't know about you and this Ashley girl? Don't underestimate me, Caleb."

William Jarvis

"You're just tired."

"Yeah, I am. I'm tired of everything. I'm tired of being alone, mourning for kids that would never grow up because my body's not strong enough for them. I'm tired of being around you and feeling like...like I don't know who you are anymore." She was crying now, crying so hard that Emmy felt bad for her. *"I'm tired of feeling like I'll be dead anytime soon. You know, maybe they're right when they said that you had something to do with Marissa's death. Maybe, this really is karma biting me in the butt."*

"You don't know that. And you know what? You just have to relax. I'm tired of all this fighting!"

She then looked at Caleb. "So, you're saying that you're innocent?"

"I know you wouldn't believe me and that's obvious. It's so easy to point a finger at me, but believe me, Emmy, I would never do that. I loved Rose. Our relationship wasn't perfect, sure, but I loved her. I know we were arguing that night...she felt like I didn't care about us not having kids—"

"Is that true, though? Didn't you care?"

Caleb took a deep breath. "I wasn't ready to...to be a father. I guess part of me stressed her out because I wanted those babies gone."

"Wow," Emmy said. "Just wow, Caleb. You make me want to believe that you're innocent and now you're saying you're at fault that those babies are gone. Kind of confusing, don't you think? What did you do, then? Did you make her drink anything? Pushed her down the stairs and—"

"No! Of course not. I would never hurt Rose like that."

"I don't know whether to believe you or not."

"Look, I know it's confusing." He said. "But...but you have to believe me when I say that I didn't want Rose to die like that. Sure there's—"

"Ashley."

Caleb took a deep breath. "That's...complicated."

"I don't think it is. I mean, she's your new girl, isn't she? So, the reason why Rose is now dead is because you want to get together with Ashley completely and to make things easier, you just want to pretend that Rose committed suicide—"

"I said I didn't kill her! Why do you keep on pushing me to admit something I didn't do?"

"So, you're telling me that you really believed that Rose killed herself?"

"Not necessarily." He said. "That...that suicide note seemed wrong..."

"What do you mean? If you didn't kill her, and she didn't commit suicide—"

"I didn't kill her. And I don't think she killed herself. She was sad at times, but she wasn't brave enough to do that." He went on. "But I believe that...that someone else did and I think I know who. But I can't be too sure..."

"What?" Emmy was even more confused. "I don't understand. Are you saying that you have a suspect for this? You think someone else killed her? Who, Caleb?"

"Emilia—"

But before Caleb could say another word, the door to the office opened and in came Ashley, looking sharp in her lacy red dress and sky high heels. "Caleb, why aren't you picking my calls? I thought—"

GRAWWWOOOORRRRR RAWWWWRRRRR

Ashley also wasn't able to finish what she was about to say because right then and there, Wendy jumped on her and scratched her on the chest, even worse than the way she scratched Caleb before.

WHAT HAPPENS NEXT

Wendy doesn't like Caleb.

Wendy doesn't like Ashley.

Could this mean that something terrible is really up?

Emmy is trying her best to figure out what happened the night Rose Rivers-Roberts died, but now she's back at Square one, and she only has Wendy to count on.

Would Emmy be able to figure out the truth?

Or will things turn to worse even more?

Find out what happens next in **The Sky Valley Cozy Mystery Cat Series Book 2: Who's Killing, Kitten?** Out soon!

ABOUT THE AUTHOR

William Jarvis loves writing mystery stories. Writing is his passion since he was a child. Now, he shares this gift with everyone through his books. He has been writing several book series and aims to do more as he grows more with his writing.

Currently, he is traveling the world while he continues to write where his feet take him.

Get Notice of Our New Releases Here!

http://eepurl.com/7jbzn

Check Out My Other Books

Sky Valley Cozy Mystery Series

Coffee, Cupcakes & Murder #1

http://www.amazon.com/dp/B00T5HOXLQ

Beaches And Coffee #2

http://www.amazon.com/dp/B00T5HSSGW

Mayhem At The Mansion #3

http://www.amazon.com/dp/B00T6G3WO0

Murderous Coffee Crumb #4

http://www.amazon.com/dp/B00T5IVM1E

Sky Valley Cozy Mystery Box Set

http://www.amazon.com/dp/B00T5IWKD8

The Ghosts Of Sky Valley Cozy Mystery Series

The Deadly Dinner #1

http://www.amazon.com/dp/B00W3T2XII

Dangerous Teas & Treats #2

http://www.amazon.com/dp/B00W3VCIGI

Into The Unknown #3

http://www.amazon.com/dp/B00W3Y611S

The Ghosts Of Sky Valley Cozy Mystery Box Set

http://www.amazon.com/dp/B00W45X6QE

Made in the USA
Middletown, DE
08 August 2020